Step One,
Step Two,
Step Three
and Four

Maria Ashworth
Big Belly Books Co.

Step One Step Two, Step Three and Four

Published by

Big Belly Book Co.
Richmond, Texas 77406
www.bigbellybookco.com

ISBN 978-1523417414
Printed and bound in the United States of America.

This book is dedicated to Dave who believed,
Aaron & Brook for inspiring
and Katy Kritique for supporting me.

Mom told me today that she'll remarry.

I'm not sure I like this guy named Larry.

What'll happen to our family of two?

Having him here just won't do.

Mom's attention is centered on me.
We like to share cups of make-believe tea.

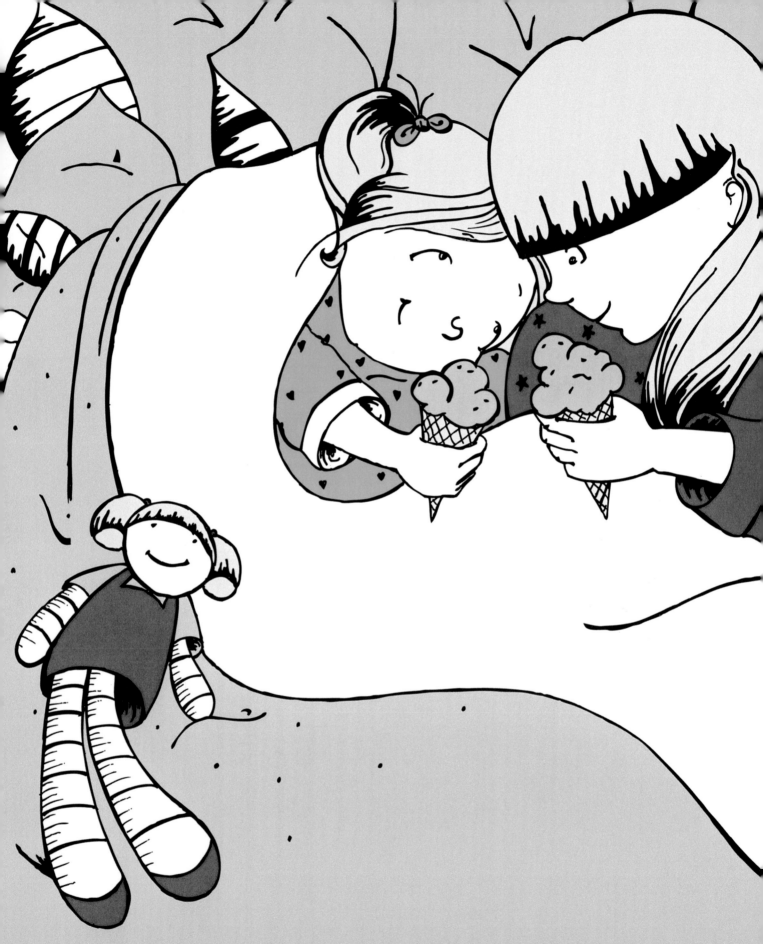

It's fun to eat ice cream while snuggling in bed,
under our warm and cuddly spread.

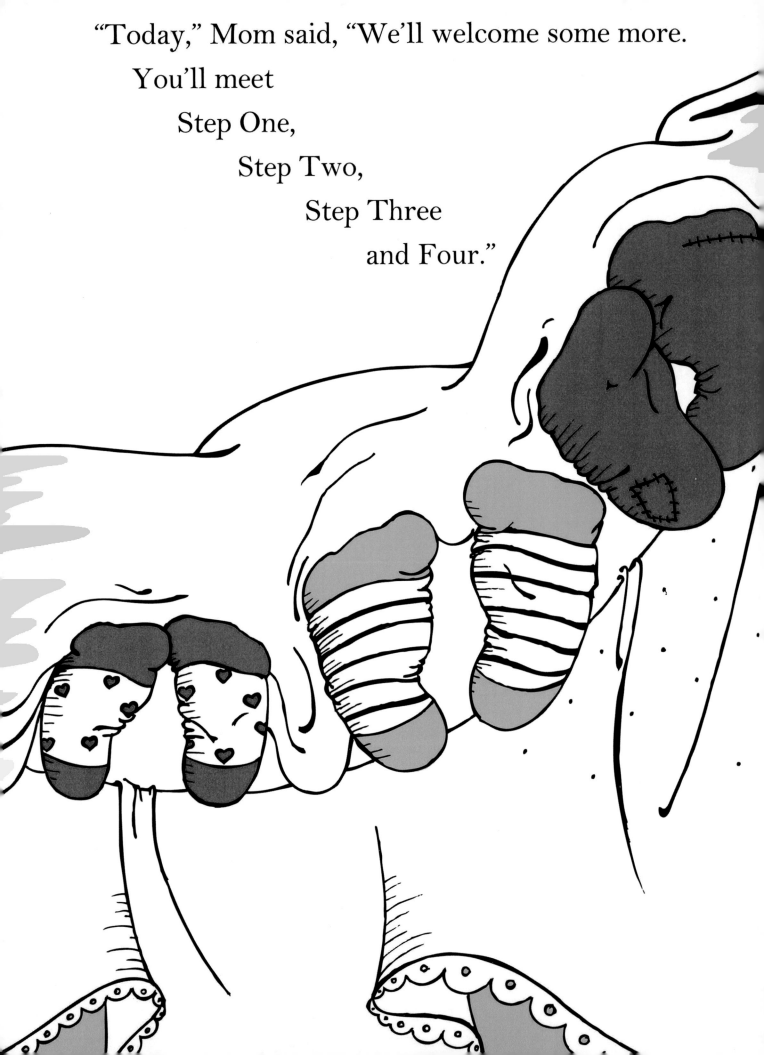

"Today," Mom said, "We'll welcome some more.
You'll meet
Step One,
Step Two,
Step Three
and Four."

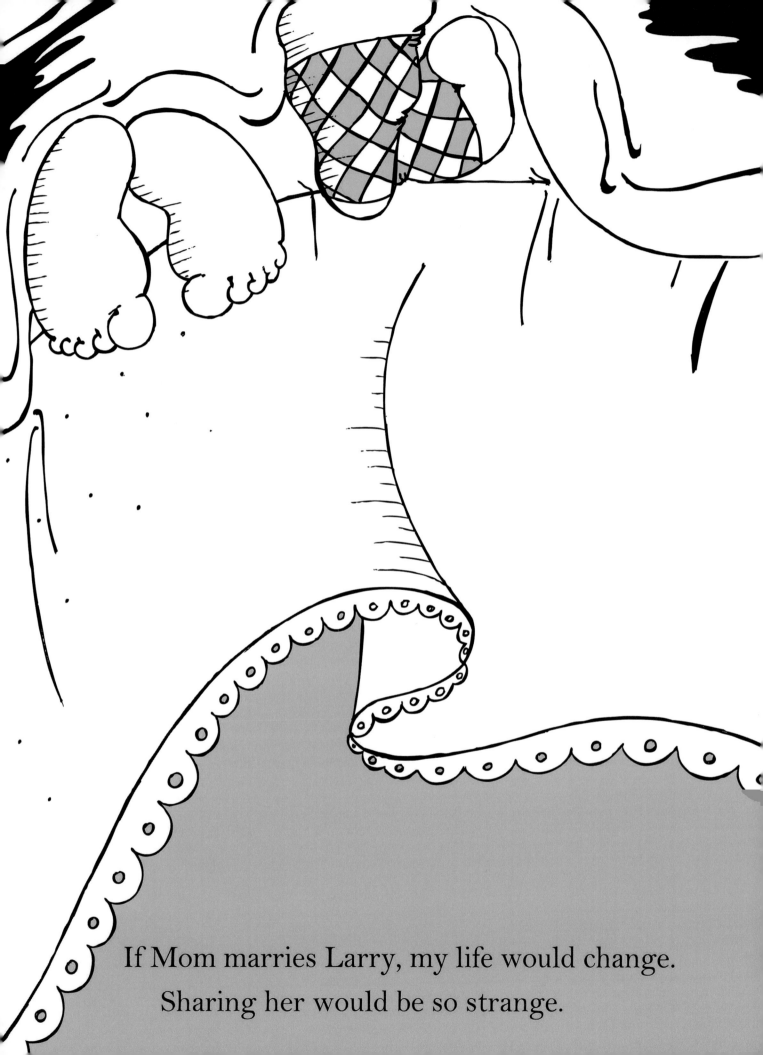

If Mom marries Larry, my life would change.
Sharing her would be so strange.

Girls would want me to braid their hair,
play house with them and make me share.

With boys around, there'd be frogs and worms,
smelly socks and disgusting germs.

"Excuse me, may I make a suggestion?"
Mom had no time to answer my question.

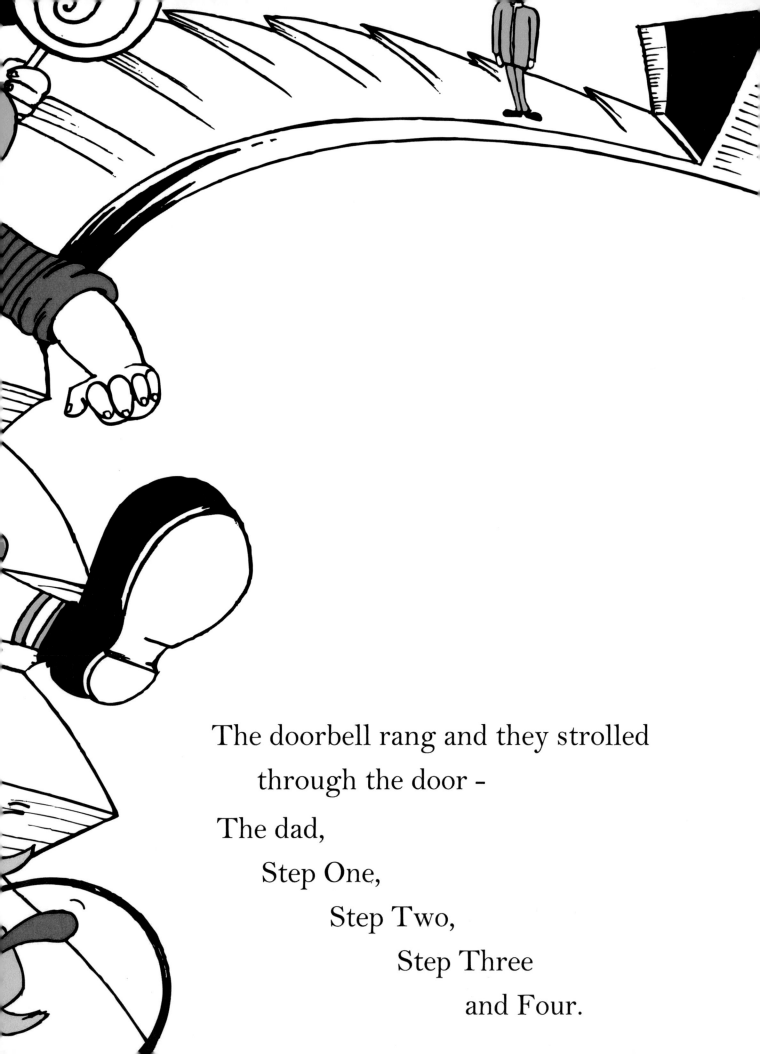

The doorbell rang and they strolled
through the door -
The dad,
Step One,
Step Two,
Step Three
and Four.

They burped and slurped right in my face
   and jumped and wrestled all in my space.
Step One gave his brothers super wedgies.
   Step Two splashed his soup and flicked his veggies.
Step Three picked his nose as he played with the dog.
   Step Four burped loudly and smelled like a hog.

"Listen up," I said to those gross boys.

"Don't even try to play with my toys.

Don't touch my dolls; stay away from my kite.

My bird dislikes boys; he's trained to bite.

If you don't do what I ask, there'll be war.

Do you hear me,

Step One,

Step Two,

Step Three

and Four?

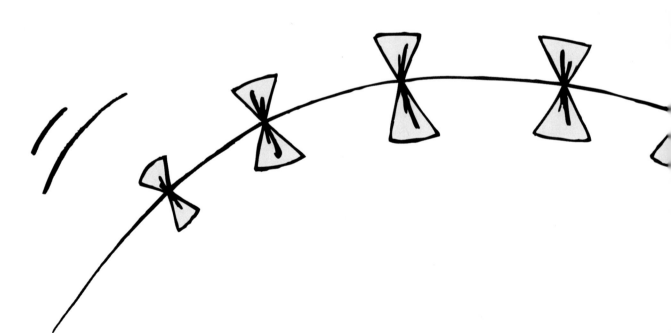

Don't breathe my air or step in my room,

or be prepared to face your doom."

I shut the door and came up with a plan
to get those stepkids off my land.
I lined up my teddies all in a row,
each of them armed and ready to go.

My room was soon a no-boy zone,
so I'd remain princess of my throne.

Mom opened the door and sat on my bed.
"Try to be nice to the boys," she said.
"Our family will be better than before.

It can be fun with
Step One,
Step Two,
Step Three
and Four."

I'd heard enough. I went out for air.
Around the corner came Ben Sinclair.
Ben was a bully and a terrible pest;
he pulled on pigtails but liked pushing the bes

This day was no different. He did it once more.

I looked up to find

Step One,

Step Two,

Step Three

and Four.

Step One moved forward as tall as could be.
"If you mess with her, you mess with me."
Step Two stood with his hands on his hips.
Step Three stared and pursed his lips.
Step Four clenched his fists till Ben turned away.
"Don't worry, Sis, everything's okay."

I knew Sinclair would bother me no more.

With

Step One,

Step Two,

Step Three

and Four.

I realized stepkids weren't such a pain.

With them around I had much to gain.

Step Four read me a bedtime book.

Step Three helped put a worm on my hook.

Step Two bought me an ice cream cone.
Step One crowned me Princess of the throne.

Life is more fun with a house of seven.

With my brothers,
Tom,
Bob,
Rob
and Kevin.

Made in the USA
San Bernardino, CA
20 August 2019